Little Albatross

Little
Alba

For Ben and Clara. M.M.

tross

Michael Morpurgo

Illustrated by

Michael Foreman

Doubleday

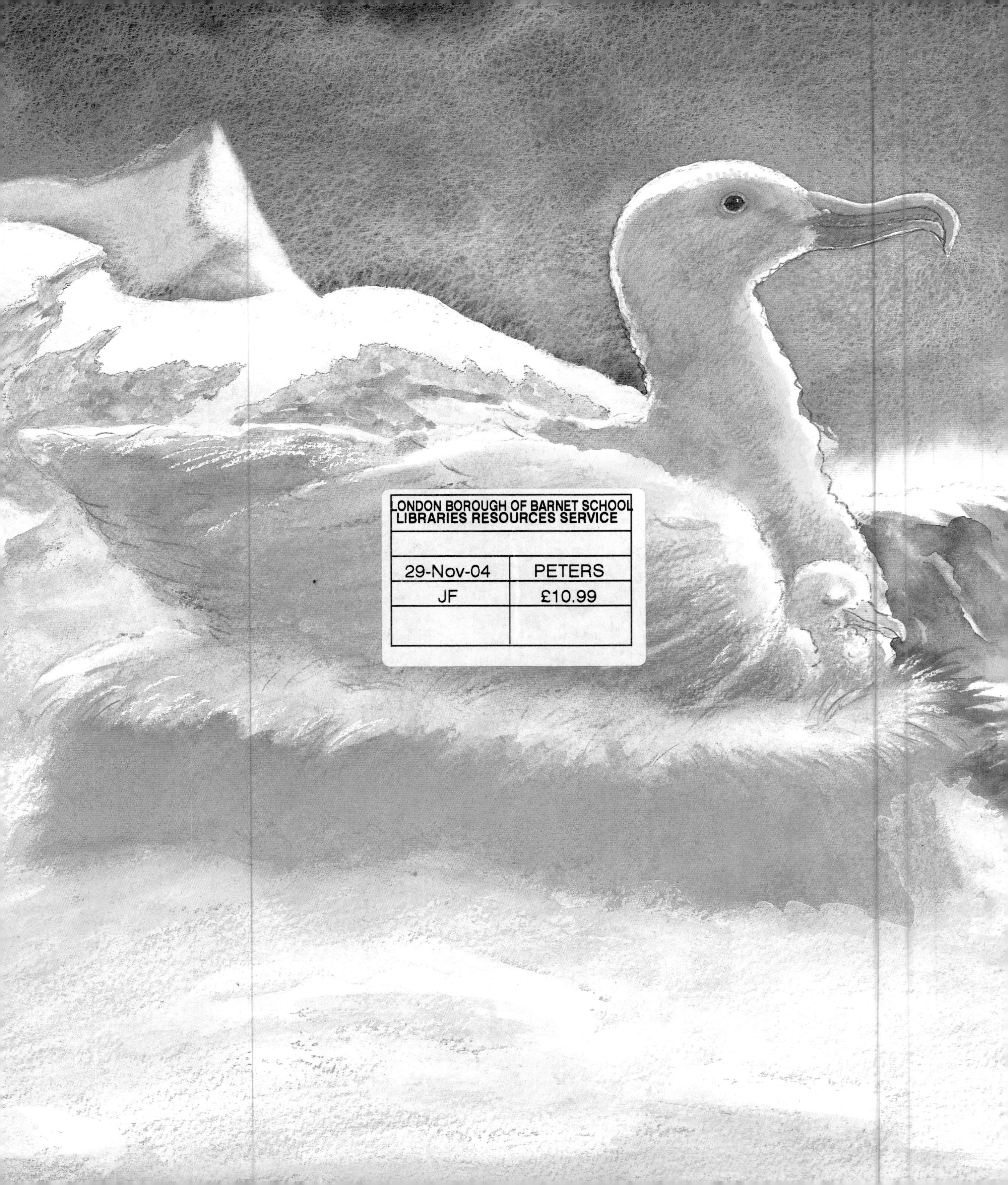

The last snows of winter were melting away.
Still, so still sat Mother Albatross, looking out
over a grey-green sea.

Underneath her, snug in the warmth of her feathers,
Little Albatross slept. He was only a few hours old,
and already strong with life.

Far out at sea Father Albatross soared above the waves, his great wide wings beating his way homewards. And he was full of the fish he had caught.

"Welcome home!" cried Mother Albatross, proud as a mother always is.

Still in his dreams Little Albatross smelt fish for the first time.

"Feed me, Father," he begged. "Feed me."

"That's what we're here for," said Father Albatross.

Little Albatross ate all he could, and then slept again.

After that, Mother and Father took it in turns. One would
go off fishing while the other stayed behind on the nest
keeping Little Albatross warm, keeping him safe.

Day by day, well fed, well guarded and warm, Little Albatross
grew ever bigger, stronger, noisier, hungrier. Through the softness
of his down he was growing fine white feathers.
And now his wings were long and wide and wonderful.

But not far away skulked a killer bird, always watchful, always waiting, and always still, so still they did not even know he was there.

Then one bright day
Mother and Father
Albatross looked at Little
Albatross and saw how big
he was, and how strong. It
would be quite safe, they
thought, to leave him for a
while and go off fishing
together.

So away they flew, out over
the cliff top, singing again
their soaring song, the song
of the wandering albatross.

They did not see the killer
bird beneath them. But the
killer bird saw them.
He was watching.
He was waiting.

"Oh Father! Oh Mother!"
cried Little Albatross,
who had never before
been left on his own.
"Come back! Come back!"

But the wind screamed
and the waves roared, and
they could not hear him.
Out over the surging sea
they soared, always on the
look-out for silver flashing
fish swimming below
them in the surging sea.
One glimpse was all
they needed.

Down they dived, deep
down into the grey-green
sea, hunting after fish.
Then up they came
again, riding the waves
and swallowing all
they had caught.

That night,
Little Albatross slept
alone on his nest.
He did not see the killer
bird skulking closer,
closer.

When morning came,
Father and Mother
Albatross were still
wandering the ocean
together, still soaring high
above the grey-green sea,
when they saw a fishing
boat beneath them. And
look! Following behind
were thousands upon
thousands of silver flashing
fish. A feast of fish!

Down they dived at once,
without ever thinking,
down into the surging sea,
where they snatched up
fish after fish after fish.
Then up they swam, up
towards the light, up
towards the air.

But they did not know
that the fishing nets were
closing in around them.
They could not see them,
until they swam right into
them and were at once
caught up, held fast and
trapped. How they fought
to free themselves. How
they struggled.

But the more they fought
and struggled, the more
entangled they became.

They were helpless now in
the nets, and they were
not alone.

All around them they saw
not only thousands of
struggling fish, but
dolphins were caught up
too, and turtles as well.

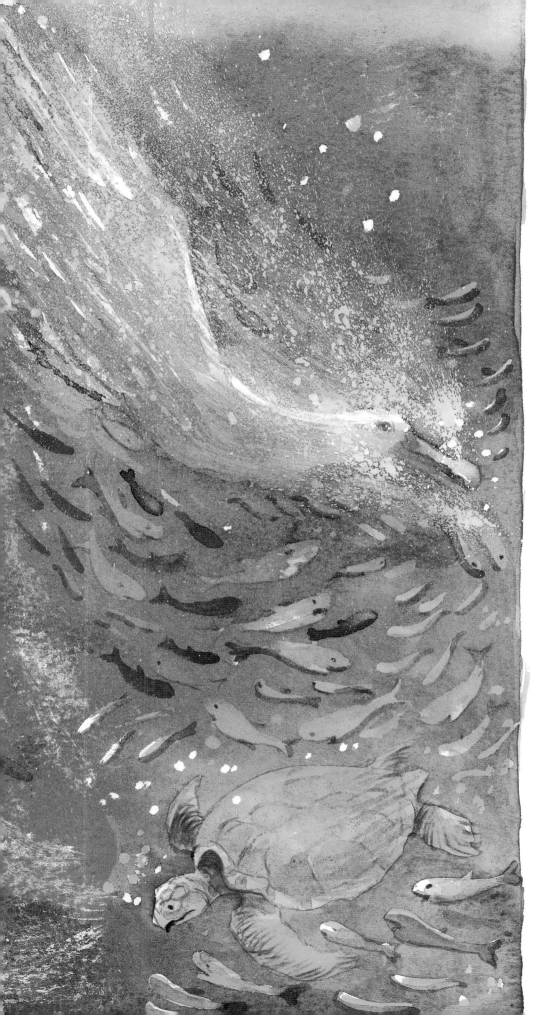

Meanwhile. . .

Back on the cliff top,
the killer bird skulked
ever closer. Closer.

And still
Little Albatross
had not seen him.

Father Albatross and Mother Albatross hung in the nets, still living, but only just. When they saw the grey shark-shadow coming up out of the depths of the ocean, they made one last bid to break free.

In his greed and in his rage, the shark attacked the nets, tearing them with terrible force.

But he was too late, for the fishermen were already winding in their nets. Up and out of the sea came the nets, filled with thousands upon thousands of fish.

And caught up in them were all the turtles and dolphins, and Mother Albatross and Father Albatross too.

As soon as the fishermen
saw them, they freed them
from the nets. They could
see at once that the birds
were too tired to fly off. So
the fishermen let them rest.

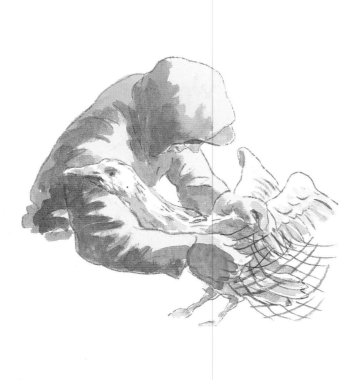

They looked after them, and
fed them to make them
strong again. By the time
they flew off that evening,
the whole crew was there
to wave them off.

By now
the killer bird
was circling.
He was moving in
for the kill.
He had waited
long enough.

Little Albatross saw
him coming, and saw
the killer glint
in his eye.

"Oh Mother!
Oh Father!"
he cried.
"Help me!
Help me!"

Suddenly, from high above them came a chilling cry. Out of the sky came Mother Albatross and Father Albatross, like two great white arrows aimed at the killer bird's heart.

He knew it would be death to stay, and flew off at once. Far out to sea they chased him and harried him until they were quite sure he would never come back.

By the time they returned Little Albatross was leaping up and down, frantic to see them, frantic for his food. But he was cross too.

"Oh Father! Oh Mother!" he cried. "I've been waiting for you for so long. I've been so frightened, so hungry. Where were you? What kept you?"

"It's a long story," said Father Albatross.

"We won't leave you again," said Mother Albatross. "Promise."

"Feed me, Father! Feed me, Mother," cried Little Albatross.

"That's what we're here for," said Mother Albatross.
And they both fed Little Albatross until he had eaten himself happy.

Then he slept.
And as he slept the first
snows of winter came falling all
about them. And the sound of
their song floated out over the
grey-green sea, the song of the
wandering albatross.

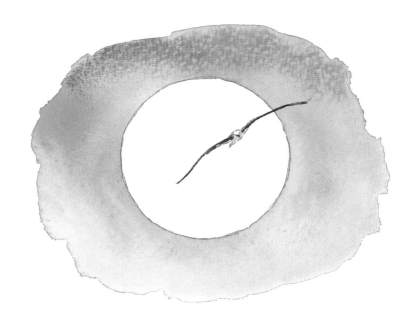

LITTLE ALBATROSS
A DOUBLEDAY BOOK 0 385 60149 2

Published in Great Britain by Doubleday,
an imprint of Random House Children's Books

This edition published 2004

1 3 5 7 9 10 8 6 4 2

Designed by Ian Butterworth

RANDOM HOUSE CHILDREN'S BOOKS
61–63 Uxbridge Rd, London W5 5SA
A division of The Random House Group Ltd

RANDOM HOUSE AUSTRALIA (PTY) LTD
20 Alfred Street, Milsons Point, Sydney,
New South Wales 2061, Australia

RANDOM HOUSE NEW ZEALAND LTD
18 Poland Road, Glenfield, Auckland 10, New Zealand

RANDOM HOUSE (PTY) LTD
Endulini, 5A Jubilee Road, Parktown 2193, South Africa

THE RANDOM HOUSE GROUP Limited Reg. No. 954009
www.**kids**at**random**house.co.uk

A CIP catalogue record for this book is available from the British Library.

Printed and bound in China